WIND-UP TOY: CHAOS RISING

DAVID OWAIN HUGHES

WIND-UP TOY: CHAOS RISING

DAVID OWAIN HUGHES

Darkerwood Publishing Group
Colorado, U.S.A.

Darkerwood Publishing Group
Colorado, U.S.A.
First Paperback Printing, August 2016 - U.S.A.

ISBN: 978-1-938839-02-3

Copyright © David Owain Hughes 2016
All Rights Reserved

Cover art by Kevin Enhart

See the back of this book for more information about the author and his work.

STORIES IN THE WIND-UP TOY SERIES

Wind-Up Toy
Happy Birthday, Simone
Playtime, Simone
Broken Plaything
Chaos Rising
Into the Playpen

Wind-Up Toy: Chaos Rising

Men: childish, whiny fucks that need constant attention and are only able to think with their dicks. Their small, miserable dicks at that — even if they do have an ample supply of inches between their legs, it's still not good enough. In the grand scheme of things, their love-truncheon is a minuscule, man-made sex tool, that's only good for being cut off and consumed by a Big. Rabid. Dog.

They are a weak, pathetic species that need constant reassurance. Just like a dog with its owner, a man will look for praise. To see if they have pleased you, their woman. If they possessed a tail, they would tuck it between their legs and cover their nuts when they knew they were in the wrong.

But not women. We are proud, strong and are able to fend for ourselves. We don't need comfort. We are feline, and can survive anything life throws at us.

We don't break like little China dolls.

Our emotions are strong. Firm.

"Please…" came his plea, breaking her chain of thought as she stood over him, watching him cry. His body shook.

We may weep us women, but we never let them *see us. We never show our weakness.*

Not like men, or this pathetic piece of shit before me…All he wants is love. *To be respected as a man, lover and slave.*

Well, fuck that!

And fuck him!

Looking down, she eyed the shoes she wore – high-heels. However, they weren't your average pair of heels. These had been designed for her, with steel toecaps.

They gleamed.

Chaos liked the way the bedroom light glinted off them.

So pretty.

"*Arrgh!*" she screamed without warning, lashing out – her toes connected with the jaw of the man who had been sniffling at her feet. He reeled. Flecks of blood splattered her 'pretty' shoes.

Droplets also splashed up her legs, which were clad in white stockings – the type of stockings that needed no support from a suspender belt. The stockings clung to her legs and stopped beneath her arse cheeks.

Her nipples hardened at her sudden outburst.

She *click-clacked* a few steps forward, and gave her slave another kick. This time, her toes punched into his soft, fleshy throat. A choking sound ensued. He collapsed to the floor. Both of his hands wrapped around his neck, as if holding the hurt would ease it.

"You made a mess of my pretty shoes and stockings, *pig!*" she yelled. She waited for her 'pig' to get to all fours, before planting a robust kick between his legs.

She giggled on hearing him gasp, then howl, before slamming against the floor again. Stepping closer, she placed one spiked heel on his back and raked it down to his buttocks.

He screamed, but didn't ask her to stop.

Filthy cunt, she thought, smiling. Placing a hand to her pussy, she could feel how wet she was; juice dripped from her folds. Shivering, she clamped her teeth together as hard as she could. *I bet he's dying to stick his tongue in there. Well, he's not going to get the chance. Not now, not ever.*

He's blown his fucking opportunity with me. I'll break him so hard, he won't be fit for anyone else!

He rolled onto his back and she stamped on his nuts once, twice, three times – she smiled as he tucked himself into a protective ball.

"Please, Mistress…*Enough!*"

"Are you back-chatting me, pig?!"

Before he could reply, she kicked him half-a-dozen times in his ribs, before circling him like a vulture. In her hand, she had a length of chain. It rattled along the floor behind her as she stalked him.

"No…" he finally gasped.

Her face contorted into rage as she flicked her wrist sending the chain whistling through the air. When it struck his flesh, he straightened like a poker, exposing the rest of his body to her wrath.

Without rest, she continued to whip his body until chucks of flesh came away with the chain. Where his skin remained intact, bruised lumps raised immediately from the brutal impacts.

Blood spewed from gashes and painted the chain links red. Some even splattered her naked body and made-up face. Blood even managed to coat her teeth.

When she stopped her frenzied beating to catch her breath, she ran her tongue over her teeth and savoured the metallic taste. "Mm-mm!" she groaned, letting her free hand slip between her legs. Chaos inserted a finger into her pussy. "You taste divine, dear!" she said, letting out an almost maniacal laugh.

As she stood there, enjoying the feel of her fingers, her slave started to drag himself away from her. "There's no safe zone, dear!" she warbled, unable to stop pleasuring herself as she watched him continue to drag his bloody body into a dark corner.

"Are you trying to find your cage?" she said between clenched teeth. Chaos, could feel an orgasm building rapidly. "You're heading in the wrong direction if…" unable to finish her sentence, due to a bout of gasps, Chaos kept rubbing a finger against her G-spot.

She bit her lip as her body quivered.

The chain fell from her gloved hand.

"Oh, God!" she screamed, collapsing to her bed. Lifting her head, she kept an eye on him. Not only did she want to make sure he didn't turn on her when she was unable to defend herself, but she liked seeing his broken, bloodied body. It aided in her orgasms, which came in waves.

With her free hand, she gripped the bedding and bunched it in her fist. Her face and neck flushed.

Chaos kept her eyes open – her slave had managed to get into a corner where he sat watching. She could see the whites of his eyes. The rest of him was a mere silhouette, but she knew he was stroking his cock due to his short, raspy breathing.

"You like this, don't you, pig-bastard?!"

She heard him groan, causing her to smile. Another orgasm washed over her, keeping her pinned to her bed. When she could take no more, her legs began to tremble, and she removed her hand.

Chaos kept still, but never took her eyes off him. "You stay there and be a good boy!" she said in the most condescending of tones before smiling and winking at him.

The control she had over him, and any man she came into contact with, was beyond exhilarating. They were her little playthings. She wasn't interested in giving them any pleasure, or allowing them to milk their cocks via her cunt. No. They did all the providing, whether it was with their tongue, fingers, or by being a punching bag for her whips, chains and other toys of pain.

It was fun.

They lived to serve her pleasure.

It was as plain and simple as that. And when she got bored, she got rid of them.

But not this slave, no…You've been at my heel for a number of years now, haven't you! she thought, squinting at him.

The strong tremors that had rocked her body so strongly only moments before, were now subsiding. Her legs, arms and hands had stopped shaking, and she could talk without a warble in her throat.

"Why do you stay, slave? It's not like it used to be! You've outlasted your purpose."

Silence.

Slave was too busy wanking and keeping a watchful eye over her.

"Leave it alone and answer me!" she demanded.

"I love you, Mistress…I have for a long time," he confessed from the shadows.

"*Love?*!" she screamed, rolling off the bed and springing to her feet, cat-like. Turning, she searched the floor frantically. When her eyes fell on the chain, she snatched it up and lurched over to him. "Love, you say?! You fucking pathetic piece of shit! If that's the case, I can strongly confirm that it's always been one-way traffic, slave-maggot!"

Chaos retracted the chain and again started to thrash her slave. Only this time, she caught him about the head and face until it was unrecognisable from blood and bruising.

"I will break you, Simone. And if I don't, I will end up killing you from beatings! You will never, ever be allowed near this body ever again. You're lower than low to me, pig," she yelled until her throat burned. "Do you hear me?!"

"What did I ever do to you but be a good, loving slave?!" he asked. Bloodied saliva drooled from his mouth and pooled on the floor.

"Nothing!" she said, laughing. "I've just become bored. Bored of how happy and eager you always are. That you seem rather content on going on satisfying me without begging for any attention – you could have changed me, possibly, had you been a bit more forceful. Had you been more of a man with me. Maybe I too could have loved you, but not now, worm." Her tone was pure vehemence.

As she screamed words at him, Chaos continued to beat him like a dog, until he fell unconscious.

"Get up! You can't quit on me until I say so, you fuck! Up!" she bellowed, fearing she would tear something in her throat. When he didn't move, she reverted to kicking him in his ribs, arms and legs.

Finally, breathless, Chaos collapsed back onto her bed. "Fucking worm!" she gasped, holding her sides. Taking deep breathes, she tried to regain control over her breathing. "Easy. Take it easy," she wheezed. It had been a long time since she'd beaten him so badly.

The fucking bastard deserved it, she thought, not daring to try and speak until she was breathing normally. *I mean it, I will kill the cunt if he doesn't break, and fuck off soon. Why won't he just go?! I could always throw him out. It's my house...No, I can't. That would be too easy. Also, it would be a sign of weakness, and I can't allow that. No man has ever pushed me to my limit, damn it.*

When she heard him groan, she sat bolt upright.

"Impossible!" she said, looking over to Simone. His head was moving, so too were his limbs. "I beat him cold..."

Her words trailed off as she watched in awe.

Shit, I can't beat him any harder! He's beyond human...No man has ever managed to shrug off my brutality before.

When Simone rolled onto his back, she noticed his cock was semi-hard – it couldn't grow to its full potential, as he was wearing his male chastity device. She seldom allowed him out of it these days.

When he 'wanked', as he had been doing a few moments ago, he had to flop it from side to side, in order to get any form of pleasure. It never resulted in an orgasm.

His bollocks must weigh a ton with all that come he's stored!

Chaos rolled onto her side and got off her bed. All the while, she kept her eye trained on his pleading erection.

"Oh, poor baby!" she giggled.

Before going to him, Chaos walked to the other side of the room and opened the door to his cage – it had been specially built and resembled a doghouse with a door.

Inside, he had a bed, blanket and bowl for water.

In all the years they had been together, she had only recently started using the home.

She also had an actual dog bed for him, which she kept by the radiator in her room. But he had not been allowed to use that in quite some time. That was for when he was a good boy, or when she was pleased with him. He may have been a good boy, always had been, but she was not pleased with him. She despised him.

"If you're awake and moving, I suggest you crawl into your home, before I beat you some more. Once you've recovered, I'll be unleashing more torture on you, slave.

Mistress has a lot of nasty little surprises up her sleeve for her eager pet."

"*Ugh…!*" he groaned, getting to all fours. His caged cock pin-balled between his thighs as he began his slow crawl towards her. Thick liquorice strings of bloody saliva, dribbled from him and dragged along the floor as he went.

"You're making a mess on my floor!" she screeched, and marched over to him. She kicked his arms from under him. His face connecting with the floor in a sickening way caused a smile to briefly flicker over her face. "Lick it up!"

"But…"

"Now, you worthless piece of fucking dog shit!" she said, putting a foot to the back of his head and forcing his face down as far as she could. "Come on, where's that tongue of yours, slave!"

"Please…Mistress, I beg…."

"Lick, damn you!"

Simone presented his tongue and started lapping at the crimson saliva about him.

"Good, good. Oops, you missed a bit. There look, there!" she demanded, pointing behind him. "Get every last bit up."

Happy with him, Chaos let him continue his slow crawl to his cage It was pitiful to watch.

"Can't you move faster!" She walked to her bed and picked up the barbed crop that lay on her bedside table. *This will get him shuffling!*

Returning to Simone, she positioned herself behind him and swung the crop like a golf club.

"*Move!*" she cut the short, stiff whip through the air, which smacked him across the left arse cheek. The barbs clung to his flesh and created shallow culverts that bubbled red when ripped out.

"*Argh!*" he screamed.

"I said move!" she cracked him across the same buttock again – the barbs almost homed in on the same spot.

"Please, Mistress…I'm crawling as fast as I…"

His words were cut short, as she whacked him again and again in the same spot – his semi-hard cock had all but shrivelled, like a tortoise retracting into its shell.

"You're not going quick enough, you fucking worm." She again attacked him, causing him to shriek in pain.

As he approached the entrance to his cage, Simone collapsed once again.

"For fuck's sake, get up! Some of us want to get to sleep tonight."

"I...I...Can't!" he gasped. "My body..."

"I don't give a flying fuck! You get in there this instant, or God help me I will kick you about this room. Do you hear me?!" she asked, stepping on his hand with her heel.

"*Ugh!* Yes..." he grizzled, again getting to all fours.

When his head disappeared into the cage, she put a foot to his abused arse cheek, and pushed him forward.

"In!" she bellowed, throwing the door closed behind him. Bending over, she looked at him through the bars. He barely had enough room to turn over, and standing was impossible. If he wanted to, Simone could get to his knees, but he would have to stoop. "Comfy, dog?!" she asked, smiling and then laughing.

"What's the matter, cat got your tongue?" she asked, watching his unmoving form.

"No, Mistress..."

"Does it hurt, does it hurt?" she mocked.

"No, Mistress. Thanks for the beating and attention – I hope you'll come back and play with me soon."

His words enraged her. "You fucking cunt, slave! You're going to be sorry you were ever born, when you are able to take more punishment."

"Thank you, Mistress."

"*Argh!*" she screamed, giving the bars on his cage door a whack with her crop. "You're going to pay, you fucking maggot. *Pay!*"

Simone didn't answer, but she thought she heard him laugh.

Deciding to let it go, she got to her feet and clicked the padlock into place. The key was on a chain around her neck. Next to that key, was another for his cock cage.

"Sleep well, worm," she said. Her words were met by his soft snores. She gave the cage a kick, before moving to her bed and slipping her shoes off. Sitting down, she rubbed her feet before removing her bloody stockings.

Chaos flopped onto her back and let her mind twist.

He is so fucking insubordinate these days. He knows, that's why. He knows I will never kick him out. That I will have to break him first. That's never going to happen. I've never seen a man take such punishment.

"Where did it all go wrong for me?" she whispered. "Could he have really changed me, had he been more of a man?"

Very possible...No, I doubt it. I've always loved having power over men. It's the only thing that gets me off and keeps me going in life. If I didn't have such an appetite for sex and dominance, then what would be the point?

Rolling onto her side, Chaos looked over at his cage.

If only...he's very attentive. He'd make a great lover and father...but no, it can never be, sadly. The bitch in me would never allow it, nor would I want it to. No. He has to go! I like men I can bend, mould and snap.

But why?

It's always been there...At least my childhood is not a sad cliché. I was born with a silver spoon in my mouth. My parents loved me, especially my father.

My father. Yes. God, I haven't thought of him in years. Being the cause of his death gave me the biggest orgasm of my life, and I was only thirteen...

***

From the moment she was born she was the apple of her father's eye. To say he loved her more than life itself would have be an understatement – he worshipped the ground she crawled upon, then later walked.

Her father's love didn't go unnoticed or unreciprocated as Chaos, christened Charlotte Ros, thought the world of him – or did, until she discovered his secrets. These things helped to change her view and feelings about her dad from a young age.

Gregory Ros, married to Katherine, was an astute, powerful and rich man, with a lot of clout in both the business and political world. Born into poverty, Gregory left home when he was just twelve-years-old and made himself a fortune by the time he was twenty-five.

He bought and sold anything and everything, until he'd made enough money to start investing in property. Before becoming rich, he'd told young Charlotte of how he used to sleep on the streets and pick waste food from bins, just to save a few pounds.

"Money's hard to come by – look after it, and it will look after you!" had been his words to her on a regular basis.

By the time he was thirty, Gregory's property retailer company was the biggest in the country. He'd even started branching out abroad, with offices popping up in France, Spain, Germany, Greece and Italy.

The fortune he'd amassed by his thirty-fifth birthday was so huge, that he could buy and sell pieces of land for fun. It was said that he had enough money in his bank account to buy a small to medium-sized country.

It was no lie, as Charlotte came to realise later in life.

She wanted for nothing as she grew up, and had spent a lot of her time moving around the country, before her mother and father had settled in south Wales. When Charlotte turned seven, her father started involving her in his business, wanting her to follow in his footsteps.

At first, she'd been uninterested, but had been a bright girl and soon took a liking to the number-crunching and politics that went with buying and selling. She also took a shine to the power of being a boss, and having people work for her.

"Can I be there when you sack people today, daddy?!" she'd asked Gregory one day.

He'd laughed and tousled her hair, "No, sweetie – that wouldn't make me a very good father!"

It disappointed her, but she'd gotten over it.

She wasn't like other girls growing up – she didn't play with dollies or skipping ropes or hula-hoops or prams or silly games. Charlotte was a proper daddy's girl, and loved being around him, his work, and his office.

"Don't you think it's unhealthy for her, Gregory?!" her mother had tackled him one day.

"Nonsense! I'm teaching the young lady economics, business and staff management," had been his argument.

Her mother had wanted a princess. A little girl she could bake cakes with and teach respectability, and how to keep a home. However, she didn't fight her husband on it. After all, he was instilling in her a solid work ethic and numeracy skills. For her age, her arithmetic was beyond excellent, so too were her social skills and vocabulary.

"I want her to have a better start at life than I did, Katherine!" Charlotte once heard him tell her mother.

As she got older, her father allowed her to watch him in action with his staff – how he would scorn and roast them before her, if the figures he wanted were not met every quarter.

"You're supposed to by my hit-team – my number ones. What the fuck am I paying you bunch of over-priced dickheads for?!" he would rant, which had firstly scared little

Charlotte, but she soon found having power over people thrilling.

At first, she didn't know what it meant. The feeling gave her butterflies in her stomach. So too did the realisation of how much she liked to see people squirm under a watchful, dutiful eye like her dad's.

Every quarter, he'd fire someone just for the hell of it, which he turned into a sport by notifying his staff that someone would be going. He didn't care if they hadn't done anything wrong or not, or whether he got rid of someone loyal and hardworking.

He bought and sold people, just like he did property.

"The looks on their faces are priceless, Charlotte. I especially love it when they beg for their employment 'but sir, I have three children and a wife to look after. I need this job!' Hysterical."

People around his office would call him a 'Cunt' or 'Money-grabbing tosser,' not knowing Charlotte's little ears were here, there and everywhere.

When she did hear people talking about her father, she would inform on them, and then watch as he ridiculed them before showing them the door. He may have enjoyed their grovelling and facial expression, but Charlotte especially enjoyed the fear in their eyes.

It spoke volumes to her.

It was especially great watching a weak man react to her father's powerful outbursts – they would shrink away from his flaying arms, whereas his female employees would break down crying.

"Never, ever let someone expose your weak side, Charlotte. If someone has you against the ropes in an argument or any other kind of situation, never show emotion. Never cry. Never cower. Give better than you're getting! Lash out with words that cut deep. Never be scared of wounding or ripping someone open, especially in business, baby girl."

Her father's words had resonated in her, as they always did.

He had been her hero, right up until the moment she had discovered his dirty little secret. It was strange, because it wasn't what he was getting up to that upset her the most – it was how much his actions had destroyed her mother. It had driven her to suicide.

To this day, she could still remember the look on her father's face when she caught him doing things he shouldn't have been.

Charlotte, I'm off out!" her mother called from downstairs. "I'll be a few hours, so if you need anything, go to your father – he's in his office."

She put her book down and got off her bed, going to her bedroom door to open it. Charlotte ducked her head out and called to her mother. "Okay, mum. But seriously, I'm eleven-years-old. I don't need babying any longer."

Katherine chuckled. "I know, sweetness. I'm off now. Oh, and check in on your father – you know what he's like when he's working from home! The man forgets to eat, drink and rest."

"I will, mummy. Have a nice morning."

"Are you sure you won't come with me?"

"No, mummy. Thanks."

"Okay, fine. Bye."

When Charlotte heard the front door bang shut, she stood and listened to the deep silence within the house. When she had been younger, the large family home had terrified her beyond belief, but not now. She found the silence within the six bedroom building soothing.

They didn't *need* a house so big – it was a display of stature, power, wealth and showiness. Nothing more. There was only one maid and a cook, but they weren't live-in. Her father didn't like 'strangers' living under his roof.

"Why don't you have quarters built for them, dear?" her mother had once tackled him.

"No, they can commute like other decent, working folk. Build them quarters? Good God, woman – you'll be hounding me to take in all the waifs and strays off our streets next!"

Bored with listening to the silence, Charlotte returned to her bed and began reading again. It wasn't long before her mind started to wander to thoughts of what her father was up to in his office. Of how busy he must be.

Her mother was right. Once he was locked away, nobody saw him for days on end. He only came out at meal times.

I'll finish this chapter and head down to his office. He might like a cup of tea or coffee. Maybe I can make him a bite to eat.

Charlotte became engrossed more and more in the story that was unfolding before her, and forgot all about popping along to see if her father needed anything. It wasn't until she heard the front door slam again, that she managed to tear her attention from her book.

God, surely mum isn't back already! she thought, looking over at the clock on her bedside table. *No, it's too early. But if it is, she'll be so angry that I haven't checked in with dad.*

Charlotte made a move to get off the bed but was stopped by muffled voices. It confused her. There was nobody in the house apart from herself and her father, and he certainly wouldn't be talking to anyone.

She pricked her ears and squinted as she tried to make out what was being said below. Unable to, Charlotte very carefully got off her bed and tip-toed to her door. Luckily, she had not closed it tight, so she was able to open it without making a noise.

"...And you're sure nobody saw you coming?" she heard her father say.

"Yes," a second voice said. It was male.

"Excellent. These meetings are very risky for me; you understand?"

"Yes."

"Like the others, I'll pay you well. Just keep it between us, okay?!"

"Okay."

"Promise?"

"Yes, I promise. Where's your wife?"

"Out shopping with my daughter. Now, come on. We don't have much time – I was hoping you'd be here sooner. You did get my message, didn't you?"

"I did but I couldn't slip away."

"Never mind, just come with me. I have an office where we can be alone."

Charlotte heard her father's voice fade into the distance, followed by the other person's. She didn't understand what was going on. Did her father have a friend over? Why was he worried about her mother returning home?

Gradually, she opened the door inch by inch, making sure she was not detected. Her heart raced, as she stepped from her room and onto the landing. She risked a quick duck of her head over the banister, and saw the coast was clear.

If he doesn't see me, he'll surely hear my beating heart! she thought, listening to the way in which it hammered out the beats per-minute. *Who is that person with dad?*

Charlotte crept over to the top of the stairs and placed her foot on the step below. Bending, she looked through the spindles and into the hallway. They had definitely gone. She started her slow and steady descent. When she reached the bottom step, she peeped around the balustrade.

Nobody. From where she stood, she could see into the kitchen and beyond.

Right, come on. I have to find out what's going on. But if dad is busy or with a client, he'll kill me. No, he won't – he loves me being involved in his work.

Undeterred, Charlotte made her way through the kitchen and to the rooms on the other side. She didn't spend much time in this section of the house. It was her dad's area – there was a billiards/games room, office and his relaxing room, which was a small sitting room with a sofa, TV and music system.

As she neared the office, she heard voices again.

There's three people now!

Putting her ear to the cool wood, she tried to make out what was being said in the room beyond.

"You'll be back later today?" she heard her dad say.

"Yes," answered the man she had heard earlier. His tone sounded gruffer, now that she was closer to him – it was the type of voice that belonged to a thug, she thought.

Her heart quickened.

The danger was exhilarating.

She felt like she had so many times in her dad's office, when he was berating his staff.

"Do you have more like this for sale?" her dad spoke.

"As many as you can handle," thug said.

"Good. You're new to me, so I'm going to have to gain your trust."

"Of course. But know one thing," said thug, "You best pay me what you owe on time, every time. I'm not as soft as Richard."

"Ha!" her father bellowed. "You don't have to worry about money – I could buy the whole world if I wanted to."

"That's what I like to hear. Am I to bring the goods here every time?"

"No. I have a little place not far from here – it's buried in the woods just outside of Porthcawl. Do you know Meadow Lake?"

"Yeah, I do. You own a property there?"

"I do. Number six Oak Drive. You can't miss it."

"Okay. So when do you want the goods dropping there?"

"Once or twice a month – Richard used make the drop on a Wednesday and Friday."

"Fine, that can be arranged. Same time as this?"

"Please," her father said.

"Shall I take this package away and drop it at Oak Drive?"

"No, I'll take this one now, but come back and collect in an hour or so."

"Fine. When I return, I want my money!"

"I'll be paying you for the whole year, and not just for today," her father said. "That's the arrangement I had with Richard."

There was a brief moment of silence.

"Right, I can work with that. I'll be back in an hour," said thug.

When Charlotte heard approaching footsteps, she rushed from the door and hid in the billiards/games room. Once there, she closed the door to a crack and peered through. From her position, she could see a man standing outside her father's office.

"Don't forget, have the money waiting!"

"You don't have to worry about it – I'm good for it."

"I hope so, because I really wouldn't want to have to bring the boys around here and smash this beautiful home up and divulge all your nasty secrets to your wife and daughter…"

"Hey! Now, there's no need for those kinds of threats. I told you, I'm more than good for it. Richard and I had a great trading relationship. Don't go spoiling it, Peter, or I'll go elsewhere!"

The office door was closed on the man, who then tapped on the wood. "Don't forget, one hour!" Peter said, turning to walk away. As he did, Charlotte slowly opened the door she was hiding behind.

I was right about Peter! she thought, watching the man walk to the front door. *All those tattoos and shaven head – he looks like a biker-type. I wonder if he's carrying a gun or knife? Why is dad doing business with a man like that? The men and women he usually deals with wear sophisticated business suits and nice shoes...*

Muffled sounds from her father's office grabbed her attention. Fully opening her door, she snuck out into the hallway and up to his office.

She placed her ear to the office door.

Nobody was talking.

All she could hear were moans and gasps.

God, he's hurt! she thought, putting her hand to the door handle.

"Don't stop!" Charlotte suddenly heard her father shout.

What is going on…

Taking her hand off the handle, she bent over and tried to look through the keyhole, but the key blocked her view.

Damn! Come on, just go in. He's not going to be mad. If he is busy working with someone, then I can always make some form of excuse…

Plunging the door handle down, Charlotte threw the door open.

She stood on the threshold in shock. She could feel her jaw sagging.

Her father hadn't noticed her. His eyes were closed and his head thrown back. He stood before his desk with his trousers around his ankles. Kneeling before him, was a lad of no more than twelve or thirteen – he had her father's penis in his mouth, which was engorged and veined.

He too didn't notice Charlotte standing there.

On closer inspection, she noticed the boy had his index finger up her father's anus.

Covering her mouth, she stopped a laugh from escaping her. She scrunched her eyes and puffed her cheeks. *Oh, my God!*

She'd seen certain things on TV and had heard some of her friends talking about boys in school, but this had been the first sexual act she had seen in the flesh.

No matter how hard she tried to stop herself from giggling, she couldn't hold it back any longer, especially when her dad started raking his hands through the youngster's hair – Charlotte erupted into a fit of laughter. She pointed at her father and the lad before her, who turned and looked at her, stunned.

Her dad pushed the boy away and scrabbled for his trousers.

"Oh, God...Princess...I...It's not what it looks like. Oh, Jesus!"

"Daddy, what have you been getting up to?!"

His face flushed. His words were stammered.

"It's...Please. Oh, dear God..."

Tears started to form at the corners of his eyes. "Get out!" he yelled at the boy, who scrambled to his feet and ran for the door.

"Peter will want paying – he'll beat me if I don't..."

"Here!" her father yelled, pulling money from his wallet and stuffing it into the boy's hands. "Get out. Now!"

The lad didn't take telling a third time. He hightailed it through the door.

"Charlotte! I...He...He was just helping daddy out, that's all!"

"Daddy, I know exactly what he was doing! I know more than you think."

"Please, don't tell mum. This is our little secret, right?!"

She looked down at his exposed privates.

"Yes, *little* secret!" she said, smiling.

His mouth sagged. "Charlotte! How dare you..."

"I don't think you're in a position to be 'how daring' me, daddy. What will mum say?" she said, smiling.

His flustered ways excited her. Exciting her in a way she hadn't felt before – there were butterflies in her stomach.

"No! You can't..."

"Oh, but I can, and I will!"

"I'm your father – you're supposed to love me unconditionally, not to mention respect me!"

"I did. Right up until this moment. Besides, you've taught me so much about the business, daddy. You've become obsolete to me. Outlasted your use. Now I can play with you, like you play with your employees. What fun we will have!"

His look was one of pure aghast, but something told her he liked it, deep down.

"Look daddy, your secret, it's getting bigger! Do you like being teased?" she covered her mouth and giggled.

He raised his hand, but couldn't follow through with striking her.

"Go ahead, daddy. Would that make you feel better?! Just know, if you do, I'll destroy you, just like your dirty secret will destroy mum.

He whipped his trousers up and collapsed into his chair.

"My God, you're a monster!"

"One you created, daddy. I'll tell you what, I'll keep what you're doing from mum, but you will dance to my tune."

"Wha…what?!"

"I'll be twelve in a few days, and there's a list of things I would like. I'd also like you to open up a bank account for me. You'll be depositing a large amount of money into it," she said, smiling.

"You don't have to do this! You know I'll give you anything you want, Charlotte!"

"I know, but this is way, way more fun, daddy."

"What else are you demanding?"

"In time, I want you to sign the company over to me."

His jaw dropped. "But…"

"There's going to be no debate. You're in my pocket now. And, whilst I'm at the office with you on Saturday and Sunday, I'll be running the show. You'll be letting me give you a good talking to in front of the staff, too."

He looked broken. His head dropped, his chin touched his chest.

"If I agree to these demands, will you promise to keep quiet. I'll never do anything like this again. We can start fresh…"

"Yes, I promise to keep quiet. But there will be more demands as I think stuff up. Humiliating such a powerful man will be so much fun, daddy. I know how you feel now, when you push your staff around. Boy, do I!"

"You evil child," he muttered, unable to look at her.

"Come on daddy, I'm not the one who likes to play naughty games with little boys. Aren't I lucky you don't like little girls in the same way?!" she said, beaming.

"Get out," he whispered.

"Okay, but I'll be back with my birthday list later."

Just then, the front door banged shut.

"Charlotte?!" her mother called, "Come and help me with the shopping."

Their eyes fused.

A smile curled her lips.

***

Chaos lay on her bed and played with her pussy at the thought of her dad's face. It had been a long time since she'd thought of that moment in her life.

Oh, how he had crumbled to my demands and wishes over the following days, weeks and months. He bowed down to me right up to the moment he died. God, how fun it had been to play him like a puppet on a string.

A powerful orgasm racked her body, causing her to scream as her fingers kept flicking her swollen G-spot.

He lavished me – showered me in gifts: clothes, money, jewellery…Anything I wanted, daddy provided!

Another orgasm passed through her – her legs started to tremble once again. She could hear Simone moaning from inside his cage.

"This is the closest you will get to my pussy, slave-bitch!" she said through gritted teeth.

Daddy even bought me a pony.

Now she was screaming. Screaming and panting. She bit her lower lip so hard, she drew blood. Chaos tried to get her fingers to stop, but she couldn't override the extreme pleasure she felt, even if it was starting to hurt.

A life-sized doll house, too.

"Yes!" she bellowed, sucking in a deep breath. Sweat broke across her brow and ran down her face into her eyes and mouth.

Satisfaction had her pinned to the mattress.

Her digits worked so fast, they seemed motorised.

Oh, how his dick had hardened at the thought of being pushed around by his little girl. His princess! Fucking pervert…

Chaos' mouth sagged, as an almighty orgasm washed over her. Her fingers were soaked. Her juices poured from her.

She gasped, rolled onto her side, closed her eyes and tried to breathe steadily. Her entire body shook uncontrollably. Puckering her lips, she violently sucked air into her lungs and blew it back out just as viciously.

"*Fuck!*" she puffed.

I must remember to think about daddy more often! How long did my games with him go on for? Must have been close to two years – yes, something like that. He died shortly after my thirteenth birthday,

A giggle escaped her.

"I loved my parents, or so I thought. When it came down to it, I didn't really give a shit about them. I don't give a shit about anyone."

I truly did love dad, but something changed in me the day I caught him with that boy. I lost all my respect for him. He showed a weakness. And when the respect went, so did the love... she thought.

Chaos sighed, and rolled onto her side.

The pleasure and shakes had subsided.

A single tear slid down her cheek.

Crushing him had been satisfying...

***

For several weeks after she had caught her father up to his naughtiness, nothing had happened, even though she kept a close eye on him. He was totally unaware to her movements – she lived in his shadows.

"I'll be watching you!" had been her parting words that day in the office – the colour had drained from his face.

Then, one Wednesday after school, whilst she'd been watching his cabin in the woods, Charlotte had seen him greet a man at the door – the same, thug-like man she had seen in the house. He was depositing a young boy to her father's cabin, to her disgust and joy.

She carried recording equipment – she had even been crafty in rigging audio and sound gear in his home office, work office and cabin. There was no escaping her watchful eye, no matter how hard he tried.

When she was in school, her monitors kept their silent eyes on him. Watching, recording, listening…

After her father took receipt of the lad, he scurried into the cabin. The thug left.

She crept through the woods from her hiding spot and inched her way up a tree – when she was high enough, she could see through some of the cabin's higher windows, which looked into the main bedroom, kitchen and lounge.

"It would seem I got here late," she whispered, removing a camcorder from her coat. Upon looking through the lens, Charlotte spotted not just one, but three boys with her father – they appeared much younger than the one she had caught him with in his office.

"What a weak, disgusting man." she uttered, catching the whole sordid act on tape.

All the sucking.

Buggery.

Kissing.

Exposing.

Undressing.

Fumbling.

Photo-taking…

She felt sick. Dirty.

Her father had even supplied hard drugs and spirits.

For the final act, he had the boys tie him up and beat him senseless.

When the show came to an end, and the boys left via pick-up from their thug boss, who she also filmed, Charlotte approached the cabin.

Her father was crawling around on the floor, trying to stop his arse from bleeding – the boys had taken turns in ramming various objects into his anus, such as dildos and anus beads

It was sickening.

Since all this had started, Charlotte had taken a keen interest in internet porn, and had done a lot of research into such things.

It was surprising what you could find…

"Well, well, daddy…I see you've been up to your old tricks again!" she said, smiling. The camera was still rolling.

He collapsed onto the floor and looked up at her – his eyes were like pinheads.

"Princess…"

"Don't you princess me, you vile beast! You said this would never, ever happen again. What will mummy think?!"

She spat on him, before giving him a swift kick in his ribs.

Charlotte was starting to enjoy herself.

"Please…" he begged, grovelling at his twelve-year-old's feet.

She kneed him in the face with all the might she could muster, which hurt and sent him sprawling backwards.

His dick stood to attention – his old balls swinging.

She wrinkled her nose then spotted a lit candle close by. The wick was melted down to a nub. On picking it up, Charlotte noticed the wax had pooled in the candle's centre.

She giggled, before pouring it onto her father's crotch.

His screams were so loud she thought they would perforate her eardrums.

All the while, she kept the camera going.

"This is punishment for being such a dirty, naughty man!"

"I...I..."

"No! I'll never listen to you again."

"Don't..."

"Shut up! You were my everything, daddy – you were my role model. Never show a weakness, that's what you told me. Well, I see yours, and, just like you taught me – I'll expose yours so bad, you'll wish you were dead!"

"...Tell..." he gasped.

"Oh, I wouldn't do that, daddy. Where would the fun be in that?!" she asked, laughing.

"But...You said..."

"I know what I said!" she let another giggle slip on seeing his singed pubic hairs – his cock had started to blister.

"Mum…"

"No, I won't tell her. I just want to have all this hanging over you."

"Why…" he coughed and then gasped.

"Because it's fun. Just like you think it's fun to humiliate your staff, daddy."

"*Ugh!*" he cried, grabbing his bollocks. "What have you done…?"

She covered her mouth and chuckled. "Well, I best get going – mum will be wondering where I've got to!" she said, turning and then skipping out the door.

Behind her, she heard her father sobbing and wailing – he shouted something, but his words were unintelligible.

For the next eight months, things carried on this way. Sometimes she would catch her father up to his old tricks at the cabin, which seemed to be his favourite place to do his nasty deeds: it was discreet. Hidden. Also, it did seem to bother him about what she had done to him there. His blasé, somewhat smug attitude thrilled her – it was the stubborn man she had once respected. Nobody was going to tell him what to do.

Then, on other days she would have him cornered in the office at work or at home.

However, she didn't confront him on every occasion.

No.

She would let him think he was safe – she toyed with him.

Once, she let him have a dozen meetings with boys of various ages, before ambushing him the very next time, informing him that she had all his delightful footage on tape.

Sometimes he would cry.

Other times he would piss himself.

But he would always beg, plead and explain how he couldn't help it.

He would ply her with more money.

More gifts.

Her tooth was kept sweet, and so he was allowed to continue with his depravity. What shocked Charlotte the most was how he never even tried to curb his ways or silence her. Silence her for good. He certainly had the power to do it.

But she knew how much he cherished her. How he would bend over backwards for her.

It truly was pitiful.

Not just pitiful, but sickening.

She was happy to keep milking him like a cash cow – that was, until he went too far; too far for even her to stomach.

After catching him with a bunch of lads no older than six or seven, she decided to finally blow the whistle on him and the sex gang who supplied him.

First, Charlotte went to her mother with the tapes she had accumulated while she had been watching her father. However, she only showed her the recordings of where she was watching from afar, not the ones where she had confronted her dad and mentally and physically abused him.

"Mum," she said, walking through the door to her house.

"I'm in the kitchen, sweetie. What is it?"

"Can you come into the living room, please? I have something I need to tell you."

"Okay, let me just dry my hands. I'm doing the dishes."

As she waited for her mother, Charlotte hooked the camera up to the TV and loaded the first tape, but didn't hit play.

"What is it, dear?"

Charlotte turned to face her mother, who was smiling, big and beautifully.

Then her face changed to confusion. "What's all this in aid of?" she asked.

"I'll show you now," Charlotte said, feeling a wave of excitement shoot up into her guts. *This is going to be pretty amusing!* she thought, looking at her mother's pretty face.

"Right, okay…" she sounded worried.

"You might want to sit down – what I have to tell and show you is going to shock you! Is dad here yet? I was hoping to beat him home…"

"He's in his office. Charlotte, you're starting to scare me!"

Before she played the first tape for her mother, she told her everything she had witnessed her father do. And, before her mother could start yelling and screaming at her for saying such awful things about her own father, she got the tape rolling.

"Where…where did you get this, young lady!" her mother screamed.

"I told you, I kept tabs on him, mum…I had to make sure I was right."

Her mother's mouth sagged. Tears started streaming down her face. Then she started to wail, which brought her father running.

"What's going on?!" he yelled.

His eyes were immediately drawn to the TV.

"You...told!" he whispered. In his hand, he held a letter opening knife. "You little bitch!"

Charlotte shrank back, and grabbed the camera, violently. All the wires connecting it to the TV were yanked out. She hit record.

"Stop!" she said, pointing the camcorder at him.

"You fucking monster!" her mother bellowed, then attacked him – she beat her fists against his arms, body and face. As he tried to control her, she pulled the knife out of his hand and started swinging it wildly at his face. "I'll kill you! The shame this will bring!"

"No!" he yelped, jumping out of her path.

Breathlessly, she lunged at him again, only for him to punch her on the chin. Charlotte's mother collapsed onto the sofa – her nose was bleeding.

"What did you do!" he screamed at Charlotte. "You've destroyed everything!"

"No, you did!" Charlotte bit back. "You couldn't fight your weakness," she smiled. Then her eyes flicked to her mother, who held the letter opening knife to her throat.

"Mum!" Charlotte had time to say, before she witnessed her mother slice through her own neck.

Blood spurted out of her ruptured flesh, spraying the curtains, sofa and carpet.

"Jesus, no!" he screamed.

Charlotte watched and recorded the whole episode.

"No, no, no!" her father said, cradling his dying wife in his arms.

"I'll be sending all the tapes to the police, father," she said, just as her mother snatched at her last breath.

"You fucking little cunt!" he yelled, jumping to his feet and rushing her.

Charlotte ran screaming out of the door and down the hallway – her destination was his office. She knew he kept a gun in his desk drawer.

"I'll kill you!" he wailed.

She could feel his heated breath on her neck.

She crashed through his office door, ran around his desk, grabbed the gun and cocked it, but couldn't aim it in time. He crashed into her, sending the weapon flying into the air.

He put both of his big hands around her throat, strangling all the air from her.

"I loved you so much, even with all this shit you had over me!"

"*Ugh...*" she gasped.

Her eyes began to bulge. Turning her head as much as she could, she saw something lying on his desk. It sat next to a bowl of monkey nuts he always kept close by.

She fumbled for the object.

"I would have given you the world and everything in it. You would have wanted for nothing..." his words trailed off. He then started screaming a high-pitched wail, as Charlotte wrapped the nutcracker around his privates and clamped them together as hard as she could.

His hold on her relaxed.

Tears poured down his cheeks.

The more pressure she applied, the more she could feel his balls yield.

"I'll pop 'em!" she said, forcing him backwards. He tripped over his own feet and sat down in his chair, hard – the nutcracker ripped free and he squealed.

"Bitch!" he said, grabbing his hurt.

She fell backwards, and crashed to the floor. Before she could scramble towards the gun, he picked it up off the floor and pointed it at her.

"You've made me do this!" he said, gritting his teeth.

He then opened his mouth, buried the muzzle and pulled the trigger – blood, brain and bone matter splashed up the wall behind him, leaving her to watch in shock, delight and absolute pleasure.

She had broken him beyond belief, causing a wetness between her legs like nothing she had ever felt before.

Once Charlotte had regained control over herself, she'd called the police. In her statement, she'd explained what her father had been up to – how she and her mother had found tapes he had made of his sick goings on.

She'd also told them that her father had turned on her mother, killing her and intending to do the same to her.

"But I fought him off, and he took his own life," she had said, with crocodile tears streaming down her face.

A few weeks after the inquest, Gregory Ros' will and testament was read – he'd bequeathed all his money and assets to his daughter, who had been sent to live with her Aunt, Sue Pass in Porthcawl.

Charlotte also requested that the stories about her father were kept out of the media, which were met.

***

After thoughts of her aunt Sue had crossed her mind, Chaos decided to get up early the following morning – dawn had barely broken. Her slave was still sleeping; she could hear his light snores.

Oh, you're in for a rude awakening, dog! she thought, tip-toeing by his kennel.

When she was out the bedroom door, Chaos made her way down to the kitchen and opened the chest freezer. Removing eight large bags of ice, she returned upstairs to the bathroom. Once there, she opened all the bags and dumped their contents into the empty bath.

She then filled it with cold water.

Nothing like a little water torture in the morning! This will sort his aches and pains right out.

Chaos felt a heat build between her legs at the thought of the punishment she had in store for him today.

That was one good thing about being left a ton of money – she didn't have to work, and so she could spend her time pleasing herself and doing whatever the hell she wanted. She also stopped Simone from working, too.

His sole job was to please her.

Well, it had been.

Now he was just a punch bag.

A broken plaything that she loved to abuse.

One day, he will just snap like daddy! And when he does, oh, it'll be glorious! she thought, feeling her juices trickle down her inner thighs. She could barely concentrate on what she was doing.

Once the bath was filled to just under the runoff, she switched the cold tap off. She dipped her fingers in, trying her best to avoid the lumps of ice – a shiver tore down her spine.

Fuck! That's absolutely freezing. Time to wake the dog!

Chaos smiled as she walked back into the bedroom and heard Simone continue to snore. Grabbing her crop, she hit the bars to his cage as hard as she could.

"Wake up!" she screamed.

Chaos took the key from around her neck and opened the padlock.

Simone groaned.

"Get out, dog!"

"Water..." he gasped.

"You'll be getting all the water you can drink, sailor. Now, move!"

Slowly, on all fours, Simone came out of the cage like a dog. As he did, Chaos inspected his battered body.

He doesn't look as badly beaten as I'd first thought.

"Does anything feel broken, dog?" she asked, not that she gave a fuck.

"No...No, Mistress. Just a little sore..."

"I didn't ask for your fucking life story, I just asked if anything was broken!" She grabbed him by his hair, and pulled him along to the bathroom.

He didn't protest, just groaned.

This fucking cunt is starting to get me down with his stiff upper-lip.

"Get in there!" she told him, pointing at the bath.

"No, not an ice bath!" he said.

"Oh, yes!" She gave him a kick in the arse for encouragement. "And when you're done sitting in there, I'll have anal hooks and wet ropes awaiting!

"*Shibari!*" he said, looking at her.

She smiled, and then nodded, remembering her aunt Sue once again…

***

Aunt Sue had been a formidable woman. She was Charlotte's dad's sister, which had made her sceptical at first, when she'd learned of who she would be staying with.

"Can't I just go into care?" Charlotte had asked the authorities.

"No honey, it'll be better for you to stay with a relative. Besides, your aunt is looking forward to having you with her," had been the reply from a dumpy, red-headed woman with glasses and freckles. Her clothes had looked as cheap as the pen she wielded to write her notes on the paper she had fastened to a clipboard.

Charlotte had eyed her with contempt, not that the woman had realised.

When Charlotte had first clapped eyes on her aunt, who she had not seen in years, the word 'regal' came to mind. She wore a blue dress, high-heels, nude-coloured tights and a hat.

"Are you going to a wedding?!" had been Charlotte's childish words.

"Why, no, dear!" had been Sue's first words to her niece. Her smile had been kind. Welcoming, even.

She may have been regal to Charlotte at the time, but, over the course of the years she spent with Sue, Charlotte came to realise that her aunt was far from imperial.

Sure, she wore nice furs and pearls, but no knickers.

"I like my lettuce to be free, dear – it needs air, just like you and I!" she would tell Charlotte, who would blush. But, over time, she came to know and understand her aunt's ways.

"I'll mould you into a strong, take-no-shit woman, Charlotte. That father of yours had always been a pervert, you know! He'd been fiddling with little boys, hadn't he?"

It wasn't a question, but a statement.

"How did you know...There was nothing in the papers?"

"People talk, dear. I had to put up with his wicked ways when we were younger. Our parents never knew. He liked to spy on me whilst I showered."

"Oh..." had been Charlotte's blushed reply.

"I told your mother to keep a good eye on him; to keep him in his place with a firm hand. That's what men need, dear. They crave it – they secretly like to be controlled and chastised like the little boys they are!"

That was one of the first proper conversations they had about her father. It had taken place a few months after her fourteenth birthday. They never spoke of him again, or what he had done, until her sixteenth birthday had come and gone.

"I have tapes, auntie Sue," Charlotte had blurted one evening, whilst they had been eating tea. She had no idea why she had said it, she just did.

"Please, dear – call me Sue! Tapes of what?!"

"Daddy, aunt...I mean, Sue."

"Really?! And where has this come from all of a sudden? We haven't spoken about that monster in some time..." she said, smiling.

"I'm really not sure. I just felt like...sharing."

"I see. And where have you been keeping them, Charlotte?"

"I buried them in the garden of my house. My old house, that is."

"Interesting."

"You see; I was worried the police would get a hold of them. I didn't want dad's shame dragged through the papers, even though he deserved it."

"Full of surprises, aren't you!"

"What did you mean, when you said men need keeping in their place – that they crave it?" Charlotte asked, almost too scared and ashamed to look her aunt in the eye now, but she did, and saw that Sue was smiling.

"Oh, I have many things to teach you, Charlotte. Many."

"Such as…?"

"Remember I told you that I would turn you into a tough-as-nails woman?" Charlotte nodded. "Well, I plan to do just that. Now you're of age, I can show you and tell you all my dirty, naughty little secrets!"

The worry, coursing through Charlotte, must have shown on her face.

"Oh, there's no need to worry, dear – I'm certainly not like that father of yours, but I am naughty. Naughty in a good way, I promise. And I know you're going to love it!"

"When do we start?" Charlotte wanted to know. She had a tremor of excitement pass through her, and again she felt that heat between her legs.

"Have you started masturbating, dear?"

A heat like no other washed over Charlotte's face. "I…I…"

"Come, there's no need to act coy around me, flower. I know you're not. Have you been getting urges?"

"Urges…?"

"Yes, down below."

Can she read my mind…?

"There's no need to look so shocked – you're of age."

"I…I…"

"Come on, spit it out."

"I get an excited…*heat* almost. Between…my legs, Sue."

"Very good. Have you explored your body?"

Charlotte looked away. "No…"

"There's nothing to be embarrassed about. How long have you been getting these urges?"

"I started feeling them around the time I was…"

"Yes?" Sue pressed.

Charlotte thought she was going to pass out from the heat that was burning her neck and cheeks. "…When I was filming dad…"

Sue gasped. "You enjoyed it?!"

Tears slid down Charlotte's face, and she thought they would evaporate once they rolled over her scorching cheeks. "I'm so ashamed, Sue!" she said, "Now that I think about it." She starting to bawl. "What's wrong with me? Am I like him? Am I broken too...?"

"Shh-shh-shh!" Sue said, getting up from her seat and making her way over to her niece. "There's certainly nothing wrong with you, dear. Did he ever...you know, try and touch you when you were filming him?"

"Ew! Gross! No, he didn't. He loved me. He was only ever interested in boys."

Sue let a giggle escape her. "You sound a lot like me, Charlotte. Did it excite you to see him caught? To see him flustered and embarrassed? Is that why you didn't blow the whistle on him immediately?"

Charlotte lowered her head again. "Yes...I know that was wrong of me – I let those poor boys suffer. If they weren't suffering with my dad, then they would have been suffering with some other pervert."

"Well, you did the right thing in the end, and a lot of bad people went to prison. I'm not going to hold it against you. A girl has to have a bit of fun!"

"Like I said, I still have the tapes. I also made him pay me for his silence…"

"You wicked thing. That's the trouble with men. They allow their dicks to think for them! Didn't he leave you everything in his will?"

Charlotte nodded.

"Huh, good girl. So, you started getting the urge to touch yourself in a sexual way when you were filming him. Why? I know because he was humiliated."

"I think it was the begging. The pleading. It did something to me…I used to get a heat between my legs and in my belly, Sue. It would be all wet down there when I checked."

"Of course. There's nothing more satisfying than seeing a man squirm, Charlotte. Did you never think to explore your pussy?"

"My, *what*?!"

"Your pussy, dear. Your vagina, hatchet wound, lettuce…*cunt*."

Charlotte gasped. "No, never."

"When you go to bed tonight, I want you to explore your pussy, Charlotte. Learn. Tomorrow night, I will indulge that soft spot you have for seeing men writhe."

"But, why…?"

"You shouldn't be denied, dear. I'll help you explore it, as I too enjoy such a thing. I'll teach you how to handle, no, how to *control* a man like a dog!"

Charlotte felt the heat rise again. "I think…I would like that, Sue!" A smile crept across her face.

"Good. And, as I said, discover your body tonight. Tomorrow, we shall talk about things before I indulge you. I am going to make a strict, lean woman out of you, dear."

"But…but…I wouldn't know where to begin!"

"Oh, dear, you are silly! I tell you what, start thinking about how much you like men to suffer, and when that heat fills you, put your hand downstairs. The rest will come naturally," Sue said, winking.

After spending a further few hours with her aunt, watching TV and chatting. Charlotte made her way up to bed at eleven o'clock. As it was a Friday, Sue allowed her to stay up that little bit longer.

As she'd bid Sue a goodnight, her aunt had replied 'Have fun', which was followed by a wink and a smile.

Red-faced, and turning her back on Sue, who was pouring herself a large glass of wine, Charlotte sloped off to bed.

And now, as she lay there, she felt her heart race in her chest. *What am I supposed to do?! Dad, she told me to think about catching him in the act. To think about his suffering...*

Closing her eyes, she tried to let her mind wander, but the sound from the TV downstairs was distracting.

*Block it out and think, damn it! Dad...dad...dad...*she repeated, and then her mind suddenly transported her back to a time she had almost forgotten. A time when she had caught her father unaware, but not when he was with boys. This was something completely different.

"Come on, Tracey – let's go inside and play for a while!" Charlotte said to her school friend, who had come to stay for the weekend.

"Why, what do you fancy doing?

"I thought maybe we could go inside and watch some TV for a change."

"Yeah, okay – sounds like it could be fun. What about playing a board game?"

"With the TV on in the background?"

Tracey nodded eagerly, causing her pigtails to flap wildly.

"Sounds good. I have Monopoly?"

"Anything else?!" Tracey asked, wrinkling her nose.

"The Game of Life?"

"Buckaroo? I'm sure I saw that in your room!"

Ugh, she's positively a child! Charlotte thought, looking at her friend. Usually on weekends, Charlotte helped her father in his office where she learned money, business and politics. She thought better of herself, and didn't have time for silly games.

But, two days ago, her mother had insisted that she have a 'fun' weekend – that she should invite a friend over.

"You should keep your own kind of company now and then, Charlotte. It's all very well learning business, but you must learn how to be a child, too!"

Reluctantly, Charlotte had given in to her mother's demands and had asked Tracey over. Not that she was that keen on the girl. However, Tracey was the one she was the closest to at school, and she had jumped at the opportunity to spend the weekend at Charlotte's.

"If you want to play that silly game, then we shall, Tracey."

"Oh cool. Thanks, Char."

"Lotte!"

"Huh?!"

"Charlotte. That's my name, not 'Char'. Ew, that's just ghastly."

"Oh, sorry!"

"It's okay. Just remember to never call me that again!"

Both girls got off the two-seater swing set and headed towards the house.

"Are you sure your mother won't mind us going inside? She did tell us to stay outside and enjoy the sunshine, Char…lotte."

"Oh, she'll be fine!" opening the door. At first, she thought there was nobody home, as the place sounded graveyard silent. But then she heard muffled voices, which were raised in frustration. Anger, almost.

"Are your parents arguing?!" Tracey asked.

"I don't know," she said, scrunching her face up in confusion.

"He-he, how embarrassing!"

"Shh! Follow me…This could be fun," Charlotte said, smiling.

As both girls edged closer to the kitchen, the voices of her parents became clearer.

"For God's sake, Gregory!"

"Look, I'm bloody trying. Are you sure the girls are outside?!"

"Yes, yes, they are playing on the swings. Are you ready?"

"No. Stop pressuring me!"

"I'm sure you don't have this problem with your slutty secretaries!"

"If that's how you're going to be!"

Silence. Then Charlotte heard the *clip-clack* of heels on the kitchen tiles.

"Shall I help?"

"You've already tried."

"Well, I can't just stand here with my knickers…"

Here mother stopped talking, as Charlotte opened the door, and saw her mother with her summer dressed rucked up above her waist. Her virginal white 'knickers' were around her ankles – her face went instantly scarlet.

"Oh…" her mother uttered.

Her father, who was naked, had his back to her.

"Look, I can't help it if I can't get it hard!" he said.

"Gregory!"

"What?!" he asked, turning around – he had his semi-hard prick in his hand. It looked like a mole's nose. His mouth sagged.

When Tracey tittered and pointed at him, his knob shrivelled even more. He blushed and covered it as quickly as he could.

"Get out!" her mother yelled. "Now!"

Giggling, both girls turned and left the kitchen. In the background, Charlotte heard her father say "Do you think they saw it?!"

"Well of course they did! You were standing there stretching it in the hopes it would go hard and big. Well, as big as it can get!" her mother said, causing the girls to erupt into hysterics, as they rushed from the kitchen.

As Charlotte lay and thought about that moment, a heat washed over her – moistness grew between her legs.

How could I have possibly forgotten about that?! It was during his tyranny over little boys! He probably couldn't get it hard with a woman...

The thought caused her to flush, as her hand inched down her body. Before she knew it, the tips of her fingers were brushing against the top of her panties – her nipples stiffened.

A harsh breath escaped her, as her fingers slid beneath the fabric of her underwear. The fine hair that covered her twat curled around her digits. She felt slightly ashamed, but couldn't stop.

"It'll come naturally," echoed Sue's words in her mind.

And it did.

Charlotte guided her fingers blindly towards the soft, wet folds of her pussy and worked one deep inside her.

She gasped.

As her finger slowly slid in and out of her, her thumb discovered the hard nub hidden in the hood of her twat. On rubbing it, she thought she was going to pass out in ecstasy.

"Oh!" she gasped, covering her mouth with her free hand, but she didn't stop pleasuring herself. It encouraged her to speed up. Taking her hand away from her mouth, she pressed it against her right breast.

She'd noticed they'd grown over the last twelve months, but had no desire to touch them, until tonight. Lifting her top up, she exposed her rock hard nipples – she took the right one between her forefinger and thumb, then gently squeezed it.

Her eyes rolled in her head.

Her moans and groans became louder, but she didn't care.

Charlotte kicked her bedding off, as her temperature soared. Sweat broke across her brow and her upper lip beaded with perspiration.

"*Oh-huh...*" she moaned, speeding her thumb and finger up.

It feels so good. I can't... "Ugh...ugh..." she panted, as an orgasm started to engulf her.

She tried clamping her mouth shut, but she couldn't stop herself from groaning louder and louder, until it she broke into a scream.

So caught up in her experiment, Charlotte hadn't noticed the sound of the TV being lowered. Nor did she notice Sue standing in her bedroom doorway – she had a cigarette in one hand, with a half-empty glass of wine in the other.

"Oh, God!" Charlotte screamed, then finally managed to clamp her mouth shut. Her whole body shook, as shockwave of electricity shot through her.

Withdrawing her fingers, she huffed and wiped the sweat from her brow using her forearm. She looked down at the nipple she had been squeezing, and noticed light bruising around the areola.

"Shit!" she uttered, looking at her tit in sheer panic. "What have I done?!"

"My, you are a little screamer, aren't you?!" Sue said, blowing smoke free of her mouth.

Charlotte looked at her aunt in total shook – her jaw hung loose.

"Sue!" she blurted, pulling her top down as quickly as she could and covering her lower half with her duvet. "I'm naked!"

"Oh, please – you don't have anything I haven't seen, dear. Don't forget, I was a nurse for many years. I've seen it all."

"What do you want?!"

"Just seeing how you were getting on. Now that you've had your first orgasm, you'll be hungry for more. But you're not going to let any dirty boys and their unclean dicks near you. Do you hear?"

"Yes!" she gasped, still mortified at her aunt's presence.

"Get some sleep, dear – it's going to be a long day…and night tomorrow! I have a lot to show you."

"Sue…?"

"Yes, dear?"

"Do I have anything to fear with you? I know you said no, but still…"

"No. Of course not. I have only your best interests at heart. Now, off to sleep. Goodnight."

"Night, Sue."

It took Charlotte a good hour to drift off to sleep. Her mind kept spinning, throwing questions at her – questions she could not possible answer.

What did she have to show me?

What did she want to teach me?

What does she have planned?

What, what, what…?

But then, just like that, when she thought her mind wouldn't shut off, it did. Charlotte fell into a deep sleep involving shrunken cocks, red faces, cries of pain and humiliation, her father and her aunt Sue.

The next morning, around nine o'clock, Sue knocked her door and entered – "Are you decent?"

Charlotte rolled over and pulled her top down, which had ridden up in the night.

"Yes," she squeaked and coughed.

"Hurry downstairs, Charlotte. I have breakfast ready. I'm dying to show you my Fun Room."

"Okay, I'll be down soon."

"Later today, I may have to take you to get a pretty dress."

"Why?" Charlotte asked.

"*Tut*, don't be dense, dear. We have male company this evening. I've invited a friend – he's bringing his son with him.

"*What?!*" Charlotte blurted. "But…but…You said no boys! You…you…"

"Stop repeating your words, dear. It's ugly – your mouth keeps flapping! I know what I said, but this is training, nothing else."

Charlotte had no words. She was terrified, yet, a little excited at the same time.

I wonder if I have time to put my fingers between my legs before rushing down for breakfast…

Sue snapped her fingers. "Are you with me?" she asked, then laughed.

"Oh, uh…Yes, of course. Could you give me a few, before I come down – I'll like to use the bathroom and whatnot."

"Of course, dear. Try not to be too long, though. I wouldn't want breakfast to spoil."

"No, just five minutes."

When Sue closed the door, Charlotte slipped her hand inside her knickers and lay back. This time, she didn't need mental images to help her. Nor did she make as much noise as last night.

Within ten minutes, she was downstairs and eating breakfast at the kitchen table. Sue had put together a superb English breakfast.

"Hungry?" Sue asked, watching her niece wolf her food down.

"Mm, yes. This is good!"

"Yes, well, the horn will do that to you, dear. It gives you the munchies, as the children would say," she said, then smiled her regal smile.

"What's your 'Fun Room'?"

Sue smiled. "I'll show you. Are you ready?"

"Yep!" Charlotte said, pushing her plate aside.

"Follow me." Sue led Charlotte out the kitchen and down the hallway. When she got to a padlocked door Charlotte had noticed on many occasions, but had never questioned it, Sue removed a key from between her tits, which hung around her neck on a chain, and used it to unlock the door.

She opened the door after placing the padlock in a safe place. With one hand, Sue reached out and flipped the light switch down. When light flooded the staircase, she continued down the steps.

"Mind your head, dear – the ceiling is a bit low here," she warned Charlotte. "This will be where we will be bringing our company tonight after dinner."

"But what's down here in a dusty old cellar?!"

"Oh, you'll see…"

When they reached the bottom, Charlotte couldn't believe her eyes. The walls were completely padded. Sound proofed. The lower room was also much bigger than she thought it would have been.

Adorning the back wall was an arsenal of lashing weapons – whips, chains, crops, paddles, bamboo shoots, sticks, canes, rulers…You name it, it was hanging there. There were also big rubber cocks, strap-ons, collars, leads, cuffs, ropes and masks. Charlotte had never seen anything like it.

"What is this place?!"

"It's a torture chamber, dear."

As Charlotte moved deeper into the room, she saw weird furniture, such as swings and chairs. "Is that a wine butt?!" she asked, pointing at the huge wooden barrel in the corner of the room.

"Why yes, dear," Sue said, all blasé.

"What on earth for?!"

Sue giggled. "It's one of my favourite torture devices."

"Oh…?"

"It's designed for water torture. Freezing water!"

The cellar even had a chest freezer situated in another corner.

"I don't think I like this, Sue. It's freaky!" she said, hearing the eerie rattle of chains, as they lazily collided with each other on the wall.

"Don't be soft, girl! Once the party gets going later today, you'll be in your kinky element. Trust me."

"And you're definitely not going to hurt me?!"

Sue scoffed. "No! For the umpteenth time. I'm going to mould you. Teach you."

"Fine, okay. Are we going shopping?"

Sue smiled, "But of course. Go and get dressed – we shall go straightaway. Whilst you're getting ready, I'll text our guests!" she said, winking.

Thirty minutes later, as promised, Sue had Charlotte bundled in the car and they were heading to town for a shopping spree.

"This is my treat, dear. I know you have plenty of money, now that your father has gone, but I'm paying this time," Sue stated, as she powered her mighty Mercedes along the road.

Just like her brother, Charlotte's father, Sue had an ample amount of cash and wasn't afraid to splash it. But this was something else Charlotte didn't understand about her aunt, because she didn't work – she was a retired nurse, even though she wasn't old enough.

"Where did you get all your money, Sue?" Charlotte blurted, knowing how rude she must have sounded.

"My, you're not *that* shy, are you?! No wonder you had your father fooled. I'm sure he thought he was raising some kind of wallflower, until you taught him a thing or two, am I right?!"

"You could say that, yes. Well?" she pushed. *Just how fucked up is my family? I want to know.*

"It's a long story, Charlotte. But, in a nutshell, I was married once. A long time ago. He was a fool – a weak, pathetic fool, who loved whiskey, horses and pole dancers a bit too much. Just like your father, my Jim was a corporate man – did everything by the book, too. When I found out about his dirty pole dancers secret, I began to get even with him. I would play dirty sex games with him. I'd beat him and leave him tied up for days on end. Once, when I had him locked up, I got him to agree to give me a pile of his cash on the promise of a blowjob of his life."

Charlotte said nothing, just sat and listened.

"Of course, he agreed – when a man's dick is stiff and throbbing, he will agree to just about anything. So, as he lay there, dick swinging, I made him sign a cheque with a fuck load of zeros. You should have seen his face, when I turned around, stuffed the check between my tits, and walked out the room, leaving him yelling and swearing."

"Ha-ha-ha!" Charlotte burst out laughing. "I bet that was a great sight, Sue!"

"Oh, very much so. He was so hot and bothered, until his heart gave out from all the shouting!"

"He *died*?!"

Now it was Sue's turns to laugh. "Oh, yes! It was hilarious. I rushed back into the room when I heard something wasn't quite right. He was thrashing about on the bed with foam coming out of his mouth – when I caught sight of his cock bouncing around, I burst into a fit of laughter. I have no idea why. It was just funny, seeing it bob around the place, as though it was struggling, too. I tell you, I've never seen such a stiff dick go so soft, so fast!"

Charlotte erupted into laughter – "I saw it happen to my father a few times."

"When you caught him by surprise?"

"Uh-huh. I really am going to have to show you the tapes, Sue – you'll get a good rise out of them, I'm sure."

"Maybe after our shopping trip, we can go and get them. Do you remember where you buried them?"

"Yes, I do. But it might be tricky. There may be people at the house?"

"Oh, you let your aunt Sue worry about things like that, dear!"

"I'll never forget this one time I caught him, Sue – he was with a couple of teenage lads, and he was flogging their naked arses. He was fully clothed, red-faced, and dripping sweat. When he saw I was standing there, filming him, he became a quivering wreck, and once again resorted to begging – 'You know I'll give you anything you want, Charlotte', he would always say. 'Money won't cut it this time,' I told him, looking at how badly the boys' skin had been shredded. There was blood everywhere."

"Gosh, what did you do?!"

"I made him strip, then I told him to give the whipping stick to the boys."

"Oh, you naughty thing! What did he say?"

"He started crying! It was hysterical. Myself and the boys just stood there, and laughed at him. As he slowly undressed, the boys took his clothes away and threw them out of the door. Once he was down to his birthday suit, that's when the fun really begun. I ridiculed his little dick, and compared it to the teens', who had impressive ones for their age. We then took turns in beating his arse until it was red raw. It was that red, planes could have used it as a landing beacon!"

"He-he! Oh, dear! How amusing."

As Sue continued to drive them to their destination, they went on swapping war stories. Sue concluded her story about her husband. About how she had masturbated at the sight of him struggling to draw breath, right up to the moment he kicked the bucket. Once he was dead, she rang the authorities and said that he'd had a heart attack during sex.

"I didn't realise he had a problem with his heart!" she'd told one of the medics. "He always liked me to tie him up," she'd continued, letting the crocodile tears flood out of her. All the while, she was smiling on the inside.

Her knickers damp.

Once they'd got to town, done their shopping and had a spot of lunch, Sue had driven Charlotte to her old home. When they got there, they had been in luck – the house and driveway were deserted, allowing Charlotte the chance to go around to the back of the home and dig up the tapes she had buried there with a garden spade that had been handily propped against the wall for her convenience.

They then made a quick escape back to Sue's, where they spent the rest of the afternoon trying on different dresses, drinking wine and telling more stories.

Sue took Charlotte back down to her cellar and demonstrated the use of a few different whipping implements, such as the bamboo shoots and crops.

"I had no idea you could use them in so many different ways."

"Oh yes, dear. And, if he's very unruly, never be scared to give him a few swift strikes to the balls – that normally puts them back in line."

After that, and with a few hours still left to kill before their company arrived, Sue and Charlotte took to watching a couple of the tapes.

"My, my, you do have a lot of me in you, Char... Hmmm..." Sue let her words trail off.

"What's the matter?"

"Your name, dear."

"Huh? What about it?"

"If you're going to be a ball-busting bitch from hell, you're going to need something more fitting."

"Oh..." Charlotte said.

"I'll need to think about that," Sue said. For now, let's start getting ready. Our guests will be here in a short while."

"Are you going to let me...play with them?!"

"In what way, dear?"

"I want to make them suffer, Sue. I want to get back to how I was with my father."

"Ha-ha, you're such a sweet little thing, aren't you? Why yes, of course. I want you to get a full on experience. This will be your first lesson in handling a man, dear."

Charlotte felt butterflies in her stomach.

The heat was back between thighs.

"I'm very much looking forward to it, Sue!"

"Come on, come with me, and bring your wine. Do you like it, by the way?"

Charlotte looked down at the red liquid, shrugged, and said "Yes, it's getting better by the mouthful!"

Sue laughed. "Come on, silly. I have a few surprises for you." She led her niece to her bedroom, where she had put all her shopping bags. "I picked up a few things for you in town."

"Oh, I didn't notice!"

"No, you were busy looking at the dresses in another shop." Sue upended a bag close to her, and a pile of cosmetics poured out of it. "Blusher, lippy, eyeshadow…Everything a lady needs to look a million, dear."

"Oh, wow! Mum never allowed me to wear make-up…"

"Well, you would have been young, dear."

"No, she put a ban on it – she told me that she never wanted to see me in make-up. She said that it would make me look like a cheap whore. I didn't know what a whore was, so she told me. 'It's a woman who goes with every man she can get her hands on. A whore sleeps with many men a day and does it for money. If you wear make-up, a man will think you're a cheap whore. A whore he can get into bed on a whim.' I'll never forget her words."

"Don't take this the wrong way, but your mother didn't have a fucking clue! Now, drink your wine, dear. I have more gifts!"

"More?!" she squealed.

"Oh, yes!" Sue said, spilling the contents of more bags onto her bed. "Try this one, dear." She handed Charlotte a black leather corset. "I hope it fits. I've done your washing, so I know your size."

"It's so pretty!"

"Come on, let's see it on you."

"Okay, I'll just go and change…"

"*Tut*, silly thing. You can change here. Like I told you, you haven't got anything I haven't seen before."

"Yes, true." With the wine swishing around inside her, Charlotte felt confident. As she started to slip her top off, Sue rifled through more bags.

"I bought you some nice lace knickers and matching bras," she said, passing everything over. "Oh, and just look at these stockings! They have pretty little pink bows on them."

Charlotte felt overwhelmed, and slightly tipsy, but she was happy to expose her body in front of her aunt, who was also undressing.

"I picked up a few new things for myself, too – a madam can never have enough nice things. You'll come to learn this, dear."

When she was down to her bra and panties, Sue advised her niece to remove her bra, before trying the corset on. "You don't want your boobs to be constricted."

So she did. Charlotte took it off and threw it down on the bed. It was the first time she'd had her tits out in front of another person.

Picking up the corset, she slipped into it. "Do you mind fastening it at the back, Sue?"

"Of course not." Charlotte sucked in a breath as the laces were tugged and tied. She felt her waist being compressed. "Right, turn around. Let's have a look at you."

Facing Sue, Charlotte saw her aunt put her hands to her mouth – a tear had formed at the corner of her eye.

"You look breathtaking!" she moved in closer and adjusted the corset here and there. "You haven't got the biggest set of boobies, but they are divine. They will drive the men wild," she said, smiling.

Even though Charlotte blushed, she smiled. She knew women worried about their bust size, but it wasn't something that she herself had ever thought or worried about.

They're just tits!

"Thanks."

"Come on, get your knickers off! I want you to try these ones on first – I want to see if they match your corset."

Shrugging off the embarrassment, Charlotte took the black, lacy thong from Sue and whipped them up her legs. She'd never tried such underwear before.

"The bit at the back feels slightly uncomfortable, Sue."

"Ha! You'll get used to that – they look fabulous on you! But, we're going to have to give you a slight shave, young lady!"

Charlotte instantly put her hand to her face.

"No, down there!" Sue continued, smiling.

"Oh!" Charlotte said, feeling her face burn.

"Come here. Come and look at yourself in the mirror." Sue pulled Charlotte's hair back – "We'll put it in a tight ponytail later."

"Why?"

"Because men like to see a woman's neckline exposed, especially if you're wearing clothes that teases their pricks!"

"I look so…*sexy!*" Charlotte looked at her small, yet full bust. Then she eyed her tight waist and sexy new thong. "I need a pair of heels…"

"Way ahead of you. I have a pair on the bed. Size four, right?"

"Sue, you're the best!" she turned and hugged her aunt.

"They fit perfectly, and make me so much taller!"

"I should think so, there's a six-inch heel on them. Just be careful – heels can be a dangerous!"

Once Sue had allowed Charlotte to strut around the bedroom a few times, and to then walk up and down the landing, she told her to get undressed and to take a shower.

"Come on, on the double – I'm going to need one too!"

After showering and shaving her pussy bald, Charlotte had barely finished slipping back into her new corset, thong, stockings and heels, before Sue was emerging from the shower – she had a towel wrapped around her.

"Want a hand with your make-up?" She asked Charlotte.

"Please!"

"Okay, finish getting dressed first. By then, I should be ready to help you.

Charlotte did as she was instructed. When she was done, she sat on the bed and awaited Sue. She couldn't help but eye her aunt, after she discarded her towel – she had a lovely lean figure, with a tattoo of a mini devil on her bald pussy.

She's rather tall, too – much taller than me, that's for sure. Her tits are much bigger, too. Must be at least a C-cup, she thought, drinking her aunt in.

Sue put on a black thong with matching bra, followed by a pair of tights, tight leather skirt and blouse.

"How do I look?" she asked, slipping into a pair of heels, which added at least four or five inches to her height.

"Formidable!" Charlotte said.

"Aw, thanks. You look good yourself! Now, we don't want to be too heavy on your make-up.

"Agreed, Sue."

"Okay, let's see what we have."

Ten minutes later, Sue had finished dolling herself and her niece up, and had applied perfume to them both.

"Let's knock 'em dead," she said, just as the doorbell rang. "That's them. Let's give them a night to remember!" Going downstairs, with Charlotte in tow, she answered the front door. A skinny, balding man of about fifty stood in the doorway. He looked as though a stiff breeze could carry him off into the ether.

"Hello, Sue!" he said, offering the half-alive bunch of flowers he was holding in his hands.

"Thank you, Paul," Sue said, having to bend over to kiss the short man on his cheek. "Is your son with you?"

"Yes," Paul said, stepping aside.

When Charlotte clapped eyes on the weedy, gangly thing behind Paul, she almost burst out laughing. He had his eyes down and his body appeared to be trembling.

"Shy, is he?" Sue asked.

"Very, but once you get Paul Jr. going, there's no stopping the lad!"

"Well, you better both come in. This is my niece, Charlotte – she will be helping me satisfy you boys tonight."

"Oh, how lovely," Paul senior said.

When Sue closed and locked the front door, the fun began.

As the men, if you could call them that, walked down the hallway and into the living room, Sue sidled up to Charlotte. "That fine specimen is yours!" she said, pointing to Paul Jr. and sniggering.

"Gee, thanks!" Charlotte said, rolling her eyes and stifling a giggle.

Sue instructed both men to sit, while they fixed refreshments.

"You know this pair?!" Charlotte asked.

"I know Paul senior, yes. He's been coming to me on and off for the last few years."

"Never brought his son along before?"

"Nope, I asked him to bring him along for you," Sue said, winking at her. "He's a real catch, isn't he?!"

Both woman laughed as they mixed cocktails and poured large glasses of wine for each other – they then took them into the living room.

Over the course of the next hour, they had dinner, drank, smoked and had a laugh, which helped bring Paul Jr. out of his shyness.

Once the drinks had been consumed and a large chunk of money had been exchanged between Paul senior and Sue, the mood in the room completely changed, as Sue became this completely different woman.

She had pre-warned Charlotte, but it still rattled her slightly.

"Up and on your fucking feet, you maggot cunts!" she raged, and then continued to rip and tear into them. "Strip, you fucking dogs. Now!"

Charlotte felt excitement flood through her as both men did as they were told, and ripped their clothes off. When they were down to their birthday suits, with their stiff dicks swinging, Sue ordered them downstairs, where the butt was brimming with ice-cold water.

Before Sue could speak again, Charlotte found her voice.

"In the barrel, you cunting dog!" she told Paul Jr. yanking a crop off the wall as she went.

"But I…"

"I…I…I," Charlotte mocked. "I said in, you miserable piece of shit!" she barked, whipping the boy as hard as she could across the backs of his knees. He buckled and cried out as he crashed to the floor

"Paul, its…" his father was about to say, but he was cut off by Sue, who grabbed him by the balls and forced him to sit in a chair that had leather straps for the occupant's wrists and ankles.

Once he was in place, Sue put clamps on his nipples, causing him to yelp – a spring-loaded mouse trap was placed by his balls, which had a safety catch on it.

"One false move and you'll never fire another amount of love muck out of your grapes again!" Sue said, knowing the thing couldn't activate with the catch in place.

"*Ugh!*" Paul said, looking up and Sue. "Please, Mistress…"

She slapped him around the face once, twice, three times – a tooth was hit free. It pinged off a wall. Blood dribbled out of his mouth.

"This is going to be an experience you'll never forget. I'm feeling real bitchy tonight, Paul. You're not going to like me tonight, baby," she said, looking down at his rock hard dick – pre-come had oozed out of its tip and was running down the exterior of the shaft. "My, my, you are a big boy! It would be a shame if your cannon's balls got squished!"

"But…But…"

"Shut the fuck up!" Sue said, putting a ball gag in his mouth and fastening it at the back of his head. She gave him a few more cracks around his face.

Sue looked up, and saw Charlotte was looking at her.

"Mm…" Charlotte moaned, "I love watching you in action, Sue!" she said, digging Paul Jr. in the small of his back with the haft of the crop. "Fucking move it!"

The boy cringed as he stepped into the barrel of cold, nut-shrivelling water. He yelped, then stared pleading, as Charlotte put the lid on, which had a hole big enough for his head to fit through. His chin rested on the wood and stopped him from drowning.

"Comfy?!" Charlotte asked, laughing.

"Ppp…ppp…please…" he chattered. "Llll…lll-llll…let me out…"

"Not going to happen, you fucking pathetic excuse for a man!"

"Thh...thh...this was my dad's iiii...ii-iii...idea, I didn't want to cccc...come!" his teeth clashed together so fast and furiously, that it reminded Charlotte of the wind-up toy teeth you could buy for children.

"No, and you won't be *coming*, either!" she laughed some more.

"Bbbb...bitch!"

"Ooo, you are a feisty one! Keep that nasty talk up, and I may just have to let you drown..."

She could see his lips starting to lose their colour, along with his cheeks. Charlotte turned her back on him and strutted over to Sue, who was twisting the clamps on Paul's nipples.

"Do you like that, baby? Do you still love me?!" she sneered.

Paul's eyes flicked around frantically, until they found Charlotte, who stared at him.

"What do you want me to do? Help you?!" she sniggered.

"I think he wants you to stroke his cock, dear!" Charlotte lurched. *I don't think I could...* "It's only a hard dick, dear. It won't bite your hand off. Give it a few gentle strokes. He might like it.

Charlotte nodded, and took Paul's erection in her small, delicate hand.

He groaned.

"I think you're doing it right!" Sue said, going over to her wall of toys and selecting a whip. She then began whipping him everywhere she could, whilst Charlotte's hand movement became more rapid.

"This is fun!" Charlotte said, watching Paul's eyes roll.

"Charlotte, you can stop now – we can't let him have too much pleasure! Come here."

She did as instructed. "What is it, Sue."

"Him," she said, pointing at Paul Jr. Remove your thong, step up on top of the barrel, crouch, and let him put his tongue inside you!"

The shock must have been evident on her face.

"It's okay – I'm here. It's just like we spoke about!"

Sue had taught Charlotte many things about pleasure, self-pleasure, torture devices and how to get the most out of a good submissive male, so she wasn't that worried.

Charlotte nodded, steeled herself, then removed her underwear and heels, before proceeding to climb above Paul Jr's face.

"Lick it!" she demanded.

"Nnn...nnnn-nnn, no!" he managed.

"If you don't, then you're never getting out of that barrel. Now, lick!"

Silence.

As the seconds ticked away, she thought he wasn't going to do it, which would make her look silly and weak.

"Sue, where's the hammer and nails – this fucker is going to spend the night..."

Before she could finish her sentence, she felt his warm, wet tongue push against her pussy's wet folds. She let out a loud gasp, which scared her. As she rocked on the balls of her feet, she kept in synch with his rapid tongue movements.

"Good, boy!" she said, from behind gritted teeth. An orgasm was quick to wash over her, but she didn't allow him to stop until she had a fourth.

After a few more hours, the night was starting to come to an end. Paul senior had paid for four hours of brutal domination, and the seconds were running out.

This has been an unforgettable experience! Charlotte thought, as she wrapped a warm towel around Paul Jr. – he snuggled into it like he'd never felt warmth before.

"Should we untie this maggot now?!" Charlotte asked, referring to Paul senior – he was slumped in his chair. Blood pissed from various wounds all over his face and body.

His cock remained hard.

"I think he's just about had enough!" Sue said, removing his gag and tossing it to one side.

"I can take anything you've got, you worthless whore!" Paul said. He spat blood at Sue's feet.

In that moment, everything changed.

"Oh, you think so, do you?!" Sue said, turning around sharply and cracking Paul senior across his face with a paddle she was holding. The smack was so hard, it rattled his teeth. His whole body quivered and his knees jerked violently, causing the trap between his legs to snap viciously closed on his scrotum, catching Sue completely off guard.

His scream was ear-piercing, causing Charlotte and Paul Jr. to shrink away.

"Untie me!" he yelled, but Sue just stood there, and watched.

"Well, that was unexpected. The safety catch was definitely engaged!" Sue said, tittering. "Charlotte, come and see this. Now!" she instructed. "Look!"

Gingerly, she walked over to her aunt and saw the blood pouring out from between Paul senior's legs.

"*Ugh*...!" he gasped, the colour drained from his face.

"Have they...severed?!" Charlotte asked.

"Not quite," Sue said, putting her hand to the devastated nut sack. "One of his bollocks has been crushed to nothing!"

Charlotte giggled. "Rip it all free!" she said, beaming.

"No!" Paul gasped, but it didn't stop Sue, who ripped the hanging, flapping scrotum free – his one good testicle hit the floor, causing Paul Jr. to retch.

"*Ew!*" Charlotte said, wrinkling her nose. However, she didn't take her eyes off the ruptured area. "Look, his cock has all but shrivelled up and gone inside him!"

Both women laughed, as Paul flopped, bucked and gasped.

"*Urgh!*" they heard Paul Jr. call from behind them. "You fucking killed him!" he yelled, then threw his towel aside. He went for the closest thing at hand, which was a whip. He ran at Sue and wrapped it around her throat. He pulled her tight to his body. "I'll fucking murder you, you fucking bitch!"

Paul Jr. was much stronger than his scrawny body suggested.

"*Argh!*" Sue squealed.

Charlotte backed off and tripped over something at her heel – she landed on her arse with a hard thump. "*Ow!*" she called out, but nobody paid her any attention. "Fuck!"

Paul senior had stopped thrashing at this point – below his seat, a neat puddle of blood had gathered. Some of it had splashed up his legs, with a small spattering on his left kneecap.

Forcing a look, she could see loose bits of flesh and veins drooping from where his nuts used to be – blood still trickled out of the wound. His face was ashen.

Charlotte then looked at Sue. Paul Jr. had her down on her knees and was screaming and swearing in her face.

"H…h…he…lp!" Sue gasped.

Charlotte got to her hands and knees then heard a crash.

Sue had managed drag Paul across the room, where they had crashed into a table holding a small tray of items. Among those items lay a syringe.

"Die!" Paul yelled, still holding her. In the tussle that followed, Sue managed to plunge the needle into her attacker's left eyeball. He jumped off her, enabling Sue to roll onto her hands and knees.

Paul Jr. staggered around the room, crashing into furniture and walls before his hands found something.

"Sue! Watch out!" was all Charlotte had chance to say, as she watched the lad crash down on top of her aunt for the second time. He plunged pair of scissors into her throat.

Before she died, she managed to palm the syringe deeper into Paul's eye, killing him instantly. He collapsed onto her.

"*Oooph*!" Sue coughed and bloodied spittle flew from her mouth. "Call…"

"What?!" Charlotte said, crying uncontrollable.

"Nine…one…"

"Sue!"

She gargled once more, and then died. Charlotte fell backwards and curled into a ball. She lay there crying for a long time, before realising she had to call the police.

All she could remember thinking was, *what are they going to think? That's another family member who's died around me!*

When she finally managed to calm her hysteria, she did what needed doing.

She called the authorities.

***

"Poor dear Sue," Chaos said. "I'd swap a hundred of you for just one of her, you useless sack of shit!"

Simone's entire body shook. She heard his teeth chatter.

"You're lucky I don't have a wine barrel like my Sue, worm! I'd put the lid on and seal it for eternity."

"Pppp…please…"

"Shut up, and get your head under the water!" she bellowed, giving the side of the bath a hard wallop with the crop she held. "Under. Now!"

Simone didn't need telling a third time.

She watched as he slipped beneath the surface – his form covered by the ice cubes that bobbed this way and that.

Not taking any chances, Chaos put her hand in the freezing water, found his head, and kept him under that little bit longer. When he started to thrash, she laughed. "Drown, piggy!"

After a few more seconds, she let him up. He smashed through the cubes and gulped air into his lungs. "Wh...why?!"

"Why not?!" she asked, slapping at his fingers that clung to the side of the bath. "Back under. Now!" she ordered, attacking his blue balls with the crop.

He submerged, and then broke the surface once again.

"Again!" she demanded.

"Nnnn...no more!" he pleaded.

"I'll decide when you've had enough, boy. Do you hear me?!"

He nodded. Water streaked paths down his face, and dripped from his chin. "Hee...heee...heat..."

"Heat?! No, I'm afraid not. You're going to sit there for a few more minutes, dickhead. And once you get out, you'll be subject to more torture. I'm sure you're looking forward to that!"

"Yea...yeah, Mistress!" he said with chattering teeth.

"Now, you wait there like a good little doggy, and Mistress will be back to get you when she's good and ready. Understand?"

Simone nodded.

"I can't hear you, dog!"

"Yea…yea…yeah!"

"I beg your pardon?!"

"Yyy…yeah, Mistress!"

"That's better. Now, stay!" she said, turning to leave the bathroom. She walked back into her bedroom. *That motherfucker best stay put, or he'll be in for the leathering of his life!* she thought.

Putting her crop down, Chaos walked over to her wall of deadly dominatrix weapons and spied the ropes and anal hooks. "Oh, how he loves being suspended from the ceiling by his arse!" she uttered.

As she was about to take the hooks and rope down, her mobile started ringing. She picked it up and looked at the number.

Who the…

"Hello!" she snapped, annoyed by the sudden disruption.

"Chaos?" came the female voice. "Is that *you*?!"

That voice rings a bell... "Who is this?!" Chaos said, raising her voice.

"Don't you know?!"

"If I knew, stupid, I wouldn't be asking!"

"Ha-ha, same old Chaos," the person said.

"Look, if you don't start giving information, I'm hanging..."

"Wow, wait! It's me..."

"Me who, dipshit?!"

"Your little Texan Taco!"

"Dawn? Dawn Cano?! No!"

"*Yes!*"

The first thing to come to Chaos' mind was Dawn's young, tight body and thirty-six-D tits, along with her shaved pussy and small tattoo of a lizard on the left side of her neck.

I used to like to trace its lines with my fingers...

Even though she was five-nine in height, she was pretty petite, with light brown eyes and dark brown hair.

"Oh, my God! How long has it been?!" Chaos asked.

"Too long, darlin'!"

So many thoughts and memories came flooding back at that moment, causing Chaos to blurt questions.

"Are you still with Lisa?"

"Swearengin?!"

"Yeah, and Tallulah?!"

Chaos' mind drifted back to Lisa – she was as equally sexy, at five-six. Her tits were a shade smaller than Dawn's at thirty-six-C, but that didn't make her any less hot. She was a temptress, who loved nothing more than teasing men's dicks with her very pink, stiff, and mighty nipples.

Like Dawn, she too had a tattoo, only hers was of Pegasus flying across her right shoulder blade.

That one I used to trace with my tongue! she thought, smiling.

"Sadly, Lisa has moved on and Tallulah has died..." Dawn said.

"That's a shame, I liked that snake..."

"Same."

Chaos was almost too excited to ask her next question, but she did. "...Are you back in town?!" Before Dawn could answer, Chaos heard the smile in her friend's voice.

"You know it! That's why I'm calling. Are you able to meet up?"

"Our old stomping ground?!"

"The Fantasy Ranch in Cardiff?" Dawn asked.

"Damn right, sister!"

"You're on. Give me an hour or so, and I'll meet you there."

"Okay," Chaos said. "I have a few things to take care of, but I'll be there. I can't believe it!"

"He-he, soon!" Dawn said, and the line went dead.

Putting her mobile back down on the dresser, Chaos turned and looked at herself in the mirror – "I'm going to need to do something with my hair!"

God, I can't believe Dawn's back in town. How long has it been?

***

After Sue's funeral, Charlotte was presented with the opportunity to stay with another family member, but had declined.

"I'm over sixteen, plus I have money – I'll be buying my own place!" she'd told a concerned uncle, who liked to lick his lips far too often as he spied her young, bare legs.

And so she did – she took a large chuck of her inheritance and bought her own place in Porthcawl. The time she had spent with Sue had helped shape her into a strong-minded, and challenging, young lady.

When she had her own slice of property, Charlotte thought she was made. Also, when she finished school for the summer, she never went back. She had decided she was going to be a stay-at-home woman, and men would look after her.

"Just like Sue, I'll dominate them. I'll bend them this way and that, until they give me everything. Once they're dry, I'll break them and throw them away, just like the filthy rubbish they are!"

But things didn't pan out the way she wanted them to at first. For one, Charlotte had no way to meet men, because she never went anywhere. Secondly, she didn't know *how* to find such men – men who wanted to be pushed around. Men who wanted to be tortured and humiliated.

So, she re-thought things.

"I think I need a bit of life experience, before I try and settle into the same role as aunt Sue," she'd uttered. One day, whilst trawling the internet, she found the answer to her musing.

An advert popped up on the screen:

Like dancing? Entertaining? Men? Then why not try out to be a pole deviant at the Fantasy Ranch?

On closer inspection of the ad, Charlotte could see that they were looking for strippers.

Must be over 18 to apply – please call in for an audition/interview

She read at the bottom.

Hmm, I'm sure I could pass for eighteen! I'm a pretty good dancer, too. It's pretty easy teaching yourself to move all slow and sexy. Sue would be so proud of me, she thought, looking down at her tits. *A splash of make-up, a short skirt…*

Writing the address down, Charlotte went to her wardrobe, which was filled with revealing, provocative clothing, and picked out the sluttiest items she could find.

After taking a quick shower, she dressed and marched down to the Fantasy Ranch at seven o'clock that evening. The bouncer didn't even question her age, just escorted to the manager's office.

When she walked in, she noticed there were women on stage performing – men were stuffing money down their knickers. A variety of coloured laser lights helped to illuminate the dark room, reminding Charlotte of a fireworks display on a dark night. A normal sixteen-year-old would have been scared, surrounded by drunk, leery men, but not Charlotte. She loved how the sexy girls were stripping the stupid fucks for all the money they had, just by shoving their tits into their faces.

It was a joke.

This will be easy money, and I'm sure the men will love my young, tight body…

"Here we are, miss," the ape of a doorman told her, when they were stood outside a door marked 'Manager'.

"You don't say?!" she said, with a look of mock astonishment.

"*Ugh!*" he grunted, and then walked off, leaving Charlotte to rap on the door.

"Come!" a voice boomed from beyond.

Charlotte gave herself the once over, unbuttoned another button on her shirt, shoved her tits out, and walked in, all leg and attitude.

"Well, well, what do we have here!" the fat guy behind his desk said. "Take a seat, pretty thing."

Charlotte did as she was told, knowing immediately that this guy would be easy to wrap around her fingers, if she played her cards right. On sitting, she pulled her skirt up that little bit higher, giving him a flash of her naked pussy.

His mouth sagged.

Got ya!

She smiled.

"Hi, my name's Charlotte," she said, extending her hand across the desk. "You are...?"

"Ugh...Oh, er...em... Herbert, Jim Herbert. But you can call me Herb, all the gals do!" he said, smiling and taking her hand into his huge, fat paw.

"Thanks, Herb!" she said, confidently. She returned his smile, and smiled wider, when he dabbed his brow. "Hot?!" she asked.

"Yes you are!" he blurted. "Oh...I..."

Charlotte giggled a schoolgirl giggle. "Thanks," she winked. "Have you still got a job going?! I'm in desperate need of one. I can start tonight." she shot at him, whilst he was still in state of shock.

"Ha! You don't mess around, do you?!"

"Time is money, Herb, or so my dad used to say."

"A wise man, your father…"

"Not that wise – he's dead. So, job wise?!"

He just looked at her. "You're a real piece of work, do you know that?!" he said, smiling.

"I like to think so."

"How old are you?"

"Eighteen."

"And you have the proof to back that up?!" he asked, letting his eyes wander down to her legs, which she had parted for him once again.

"If I don't?"

"Oh, well…" he said, his eyes glued to her crotch. "I'm sure we can work something out. Can you come down tomorrow? Do a few dance routines. I'd like to see you how you move!"

I'm sure you would, you dirty old cunt.

"Sure! Shall we say five?"

"Make it four – we like to run a few hours before we get going."

"I'll be here," she said.

"Hey, and change that name of yours! We can't have a gorgeous thing like you up on that stage with such a name.

Bring your tight arse and new name around tomorrow at four. I'll be waiting to greet you by the door."

"You got it," she winked, and then headed out the door.

That night, after a long, hot soak in the tub, a delicious pasta meal and a few large glasses of wine, Charlotte sat down and run through a load of names.

"It has to be something catchy!" she uttered, turning her music down low and taking a glug of wine. She had a pen and pad by her side.

"Raven!" she said, writing it down. "After all, I do have thick, black hair. I could wear my leather suits on stage…No, wait – I'll be a stripper. Less is best."

Putting a scratch through Raven, she wrote a few more down:

Raven

Amber

Destruction

Destroyer

Deviant

Foxy

~~Amber~~

~~Cherry~~

Hmm, I do kind of like Destruction and Deviant...They kind of sum me up, she thought, tapping her pen against her pad. *Think damn it, think!*

"What about my own name!"

She scribbled her name down on the pad and picked letters out to try and form a name.

~~Char~~

~~Lotte~~

~~Ros~~

"Damn it, I've never been any good with words!" she said, slamming her pen down, and that's when she saw it.

That's it!

Chaos

"Chaos," she said, letting it roll off her tongue. "It's perfect. From this day forward, that's what I will be known as!"

Once she had her chosen name, Chaos decided to turn the music up high and get blind drunk.

"Not like I have anywhere to be early in the morning!"

The next day, Chaos awoke with a stinking headache.

Ugh…It feels as though there's a brass band going for it inside my head!

Undeterred, she got up and prepped herself for the day ahead. She started proceedings by going for a long jog, followed by a boiling hot shower, a full English breakfast and two mugs of strong coffee.

"Don't think I'll wait until three-thirty to make my way down there," she spoke aloud. "I'll get there for three. I want to make a good impression!" she decided, clearing her breakfast things away and pouring herself a third coffee.

With her hot drink in hand, she sat in front of the TV and listened to the news as she drained the last of her coffee. Once done, she put the mug in the kitchen and went upstairs to get dressed. She also packed a sports bag full of other clothes, including clean underwear, make-up and energy drinks.

"You never know!"

Once ready, she picked her bag up off her bed and checked herself in the mirror. She'd chosen her old school uniform, which consisted of a tight, white shirt, a short, pleated skirt, knee-high socks, sensible shoes and tie. Chaos had also put her luscious black hair into pigtails.

She was braless, and her nipples poked at the thin fabric of her shirt.

"And, to complete the look!" she said, popping chewing gum into her mouth, she snapped a few bubbles. "Perfect."

With a nod, she turned around and left the house.

Within twenty minutes, she was standing outside the locked doors of the Fantasy Ranch.

"Damn, maybe this wasn't such a grand fucking idea!" she said, giving the door a few hard thumps. "Come on, open up."

At her back, a car full of men drove by, and started shouting, heckling and whistling at her.

She turned around, and yelled "Fuck off!" whilst giving them the middle finger. "Arseholes!" she uttered. When she turned back to the door, she heard the locks disengage.

"Who the fuck is it?!" Chaos heard Herb say, before the door flew open. "Oh, Charlotte! You're way too early," he said, looking at his watch.

"I know," she said, turning her torso this way and that, causing her skirt to flap.

She had his attention.

"I thought I'd come down early, you know – show how keen I am!" she snapped her gum and gave him a wink. "Also, I thought I could give you a private show, if you know what I mean!"

"Oh, well…"

"But, if it's a problem, I can always come back later," she said, pouting and lowering her head.

"No, no, no!" he protested. "Come in, please."

"Are you sure?!"

"Of course."

"Thanks," she said, walking through the door. The club smelt of stale booze and cigarettes, but everything was clean – the bar, stage and tables. "The cleaners have already been and gone?"

"Yep. Now, how about that private dance?!" he asked, pawing at her shoulder.

Fighting the vomit back, she nodded. "Of course. You sit yourself down there, and I'll get started!"

On turning, she saw him grin. "Sure!" he said, taking up a chair close to the stage. "If you can impress me, I'll give you the job here and now."

"Excellent."

"What are you doing?" he asked, watching Chaos set up a camcorder.

"I want to record my performance for my portfolio," she lied. *Oh, you'll be giving me a job, ya fat piece of shit.*

"Okay."

When she was ready, Chaos started writhing and shaking her small arse. Her petite tits bobbed and almost popped free of her loosely buttoned shirt, as she strutted across the stage. As her routine progressed, off came her clothes, until she was naked, apart from a thong.

"So, what do you think? Do I have the moves?"

"Well, why don't you show me that pretty twat of yours and I'll consider it!"

"Hey! You just wanted a dance."

"Come on now, show me," he said, getting out of his chair. "You do want a job, don't you?" he said, smiling.

"Yes, and you're going to give me one."

"I don't have to give you shit, bitch! You came flouncing in here…"

Before he could drive his point home, Chaos got off the stage and grabbed her stuff, along with the camera.

"Fine," she said. "Ill be off, and I'll be taking this tape to the police – I'll tell them how you tried to rape and seduce a minor," she said, smiling.

His face reddened. She saw his jaw muscles flex.

"Bye, then!" she said, walking towards the door.

"*Wait!*"

"Yes?" she said, turning to face him.

"You can start tonight! How the fuck did you know?!"

"Know what, Herb?"

"That I wasn't going to hire you – that I was hoping…"

"Hoping for a cheap screw? That you would get me down here just to fuck me and then tell me to piss off?!"

"Yes!" he said from behind gritted teeth.

"Huh," she huffed. "You're a man – I can see right fucking through you! I'll be back in a few hours. Don't worry, I'll be here for my first show." Winking at him, Chaos strut towards the door. "Oh, and Herb?"

"Yeah?!"

"My new name is Chaos, chick. You better make sure I do have a job when I return, or I am going to the police."

"Don't worry, you got my attention!" he said, smiling and shaking his head. "You truly are some piece of work. When you get here later, report to Dawn Cano – she goes by The Dark Delight. She's the head dancer, and looks after you girls."

"Thanks, I will!"

That night, on returning to the Fantasy Ranch, Chaos caught up with Dawn - The Dark Delight - Cano, after she was told by the barman that her dance instructor was up on stage, 'doing her thing'.

On approaching the stage, Chaos could see two women dancing closely. Their naked bodies touching – their stiffened nipples collided. Wrapped around the body of the shorter of the two, who Chaos came to know as Lisa, Ice Killer, Swearengin, was a fat-bodied boa constrictor.

As their faces got closer to one another, their tongues emerged and tangled in a lover's knot, which Chaos found extremely hot.

When the music finally came to an end, Dawn left the stage and addressed her.

"So, you're the newbie, huh? You look like a kid! But hey, you've got great tits. Herb has an eye for talent. Why don't you get your scrawny arse up here, and show me what you can do!"

Chaos found her bluntness irresistible, and soon a long and lasting friendship started, until Chaos left the company a few years later, after she met Simone in a dominatrix club in Cardiff.

***

When Chaos was dressed and ready for her rendezvous with her old friend, she ordered her slave out of the bath and made him dress.

"Looks like you've been saved by the bell, maggot!"

"Hhh…how so, mmm…Mistress?!"

"I have to go out, and I'm going to be gone for a few hours, but I'll be sure to continue the torture once I'm home!" she said, smiling.

"Pppp…permission to have some time out of the house, Mistress? I nnn…need some fresh air!"

She thought about this for a moment. "Where will you go?!"

"I www…was going to go down to the fair…"

"If I allow this, I want you back by eight. Do you hear me?!"

He nodded, "Yea…yes, Mistress. I only want an hour or so, just to stretch…"

"Shut up, maggot!" she said, slapping him across the face. "You may have your time out," she said, looking down at his caged cock. "You stay out of trouble. And, if I have to come looking for you, there will be hell to pay!"

Again, he nodded. "Yes, Mistress."

"Good, now go and do what you have to. I'm off now, so behave!" she said, leaving the bedroom. As she got to the door, she thought she heard him giggle. She turned on her heel. "Something funny, slave?"

"No, Mistress. I didn't say or do anything…" he said, laughing hard on the inside, as he watched her leave him all alone.

***

Simone smiled at her back, and thought, *this is my chance to escape*... "I'll show you, bitch!" he whispered, then prepared to leave the house for the evening...

FINIS

ABOUT THE AUTHOR

David Owain Hughes is a horror freak! He grew up on ninja, pirate and horror movies from the age of five, which helped rapidly install in him a vivid imagination. When he grows up, he wishes to be a serial killer with a part-time job in women's lingerie…He's had several short stories published in various online magazines and anthologies, along with articles, reviews and interviews. He's written for This Is Horror, Blood Magazine and Horror Geeks Magazine. He's the author of the popular novels "Walled In" (2014) and "Wind-Up Toy" (2016), along with his short story collections "White Walls and Straitjackets" (2015) and "Choice Cuts" (2015).

LINKS

Facebook: www.facebook.com/DOHughesAuthor/?ref=hl

Twitter: DOHUGHES32

Website: http://david-owain-hughes.wix.com/horrorwriter

www.ingramcontent.com/pod-product-compliance
Lightning Source LLC
Chambersburg PA
CBHW070602180626
46817CB00005B/1953